THIS IS NOT A DRILL

THIS IS NOT A DRILL

K.A. HOLT

Scholastic Press
New York

Library of Congress Cataloging-in-Publication Data available

ISBN 978-1-338-73958-9

1 2021

Printed in the U.S.A.   23
First edition, March 2022

Book design by Christopher Stengel

CV 12.20.2021 0339

For Joan, without whom my fruit cocktails would have no cherries

Battery 46%

NATIONAL NEWS NOW: Multiple llamas escape transport van, cause small-town chaos!

LOCAL NEWS TODAY: See a llama on your commute this morning? You're not the only one. Police ask vehicles to avoid downtown area.

TEENBUZZ: Five lip-plumping shades to make him finally notice your smile!

LILA O'LOWRY MIDDLE SCHOOL APP: It has been 213 days since you last checked the LOLMS app.

500+ UNREAD LOLMS NOTIFICATIONS

CHAR: Wakey, wakey! Feeling better this morning?

MAMABEAR: Text me when you're up.

5+ UNREAD TEXTS

Morning, early bird.

CHAR

She's awake! hallelellluhuahgahah!

So cruel to start school when it's basically still nighttime.

MorningNight™ is for sleeping.

CHAR

Morning is the best part of the day!

Nothing has gone wrong yet!

Think about it. Mornings are like the Mondays of the day!

Omg, Char. No.

Everyone hates Mondays

CHAR

I think people just say they hate Mondays because that's what *everyone* says.

Also, today is Thursday.

I know today is Thursday!

How can u txt in full sentences when it's this early?

Or on a flip phone for that matter.

How can u even txt in full WORDS this early on a flip phone?

omg 46%???

Whyyyy do I always forget to plug in my phone at night aaaarrrrrgghh

CHAR

You know I can't see emojis.

This magical flip phone just says omg 46%??? [angry face]

But also this magical flip phone has a battery that lasts for dayzzzzz, so . . .

But also, also I bet flip texting feels like [hamster wheel emoji].

CHAR

There's a hamster wheel emoji??

Haha. No. I just wrote it out to see what it feels like to write out emojis. I don't like it.

CHAR

I feel like I'm on a hamster wheel all the time.

That is just how I do.

[shrugging Char emoji]

Omg, char, GET A PHONE WITH EMOJIS

CHAR

No way Moppa will let me.

Plus, I'm kind of proud of my fast hamster wheel texting.

A skill not many have.

AND it's pretty awesome to have an unlimited, incredibly specific library of emojis.

Did you just call your BRAIN an unlimited library of emojis?? askjghakjsgh

😉 I don't think it counts as an emoji if you make it up and spell it out?

CHAR

[Char is scrolling through her unlimited library of emojis emoji]

[Char sticks her tongue out at Ava emoji]

Meanwhile im growing a beard waiting for ur txts.

CHAR

Where is E on this fine morning?

Eeeeee

Elenaaaaaaa

You know how her dad is about phones before school.

CHAR

I'd be that way, too, if I had to get E awake and moving before noon.

[sleeping emoji] [sloth emoji] [that one picture of E from last summer at the cabin]

[the one where she was still sound asleep at like 2 PM]

[with her mouth hanging open]

💀 ajhgshjdfgldsg

CHAR

No offense, E!

We love your lazy booty, E!

Omg speaking of lazy booties, HOW have I been just laying here for 30 minutes???

CHAR

Lying.

WHAT. I'm not LYING!

CHAR

Yes you are. You're lying in bed. You can only LAY in bed if someone places you there. Like an Ava-shaped sloth pillow.

OMG 🙄

I have to get up and get dressed

CHAR

OMG [eye roll emoji] did you just get a push from the app?

Probably? I get so many they're basically invisible now.

Why? Was it URGENT?

CHAR

[Char laughing emoji]

Yeah. URGENT! Check the app for today's lunch menu so you don't starve and die.

adsjhsdg 💀 it did not say that

CHAR

You could verify my truthiness IF ONLY YOUR NOTIFICATIONS WEREN'T INVISIBLE!

(or you could, idk, check the app)

Or YOU could check the app.

Except you can't on that 🤓 flip phone, can you?

CHAR

No apps, and yet somehow I still get notifications texted to me.

[Char shrugging and crying emoji] It's the worst of all worlds.

I bet you 265823509 million dollars the app just says FRUIT COCKTAIL

FRUIT COCKTAIL

FRUIT COCKTAIL

CHAR

That's a lot of millions of dollars, so I will take that bet.

Hold please.

LOLMS GLOBAL ANNOUNCEMENTS

Today's Lunch! Grilled cheese. Tomato soup. Green beans. Fruit cocktail.

Posted an hour ago. Comments turned off on this post

Today's Lunch! Steak fingers. Baked potato. Peas and corn medley. Fruit cocktail.

Posted one day ago. Comments turned off on this post

Today's Lunch! Fish fillet. Macaroni and cheese. Broccoli florets. Fruit cocktail.

Posted two days ago. Comments turned off on this post

Today's Lunch! Pizza. Corn on the cob. Green beans. Fruit cocktail.

Posted three days ago. Comments turned off on this post

Today's Lunch! Chicken patty. Roasted vegetables. Rice medley. Fruit cocktail.

Posted last week. Comments turned off on this post

Today's Lunch! Beef enchiladas. Charro beans. Green salad. Fruit cocktail.

Posted last week. Comments turned off on this post

Today's Lunch! Grilled cheese. Tomato soup. Green beans. Fruit cocktail.

Posted last week. Comments turned off on this post

[more]

(175) new messages

LOLMS COMMUNITY CORKBOARD

Chase M. Hello? Anyone here? How do I buy a t-shirt for PE?

Dwayne R. Smell my pits, Chase.

(2) new messages

AVA'S CLASSROOM ANNOUNCEMENTS

US History test tomorrow!

South American river map due tomorrow!

Algebra quiz on Monday!

(225) new messages

E & CHAR

Today 6:43 AM

I was 100% A+ correct! All very urgent fruit cocktail announcements.

CHAR

How dare you question the urgency of fruit cocktail?

How

Dare

You

dasjhfgkajsgfhjf 💀 I believe you owe me lots of millions of dollars now.

CHAR

You keep doing that, but what is it? [laughing skull emoji?]

CHAR GET A PHONE WITH EMOJIS AND YOU WILL UNDERSTAND 💀

CHAR

MOPPA WON'T LET ME!

I AM STILL NOT DRESSED!!

CHAR

YOU BETTER HURRY!

See you out front in 10?

CHAR

[thumbs up emoji]

Oh, hey, can you bring that comic you borrowed from BabyD?

Which comic? I borrowed a jillion. Ms. Marvel? Runaways? The one with the lions?

CHAR

Idk. All he said was to ask if you were done because he wants to let Chase borrow it.

I finished Ms. Marvel last night. I'll bring that one.

CHAR

A) I still think it's weird that you borrow comics from my little brother.

B) He better get ready fast if he's walking with us.

B 1/2) I'll tell him about Ms. Marvel.

C) See you in 8.

Ok

MAMABEAR

Today 6:51 AM

MAMABEAR

Good morning, kiddo! Love you! See you after school!

Sorry I missed you this morning.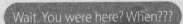

Wait. You were here? When???

MAMABEAR

Had to run by the house super quick. I didn't want it to be A Thing, so Dad put the stuff I needed in the garage.

It's still your house, too, you know.

MAMABEAR

I know. Your dad does, too! I'm just trying to make things easier.

Ava?

Kiddo?

It's all going to be ok. I promise.

Better, even!

I'll pick you up at the Gas N Sip after school.

We can grab some ice cream and talk it out.

Love you.

7:50 AM

Battery 41%

NATIONAL NEWS NOW: Two escaped llamas hold small-town drivers hostage. THIS IS A DEVELOPING STORY.

LOCAL NEWS TODAY: Llama drama continues as Main Street remains closed to vehicles.

TEENBUZZ: Experts weigh in on top communication strategies for teens. HINT: He can't read your mind, ladies!

500+ UNREAD LOLMS NOTIFICATIONS

OMGGG 41%

E, do you have a charger I can borrow at lunch?

Grrrrrl, where are you? Late bell just rang.

E

Go tell Ms. Abernathy not to mark me absent! I'm on my way!

For once it's not my fault that I'm running late.

There were LLAMAS in the street.

Like, WHAT! ACTUAL LLAMAS, happy as can be running in and out of traffic.

I thought I was still dreaming or something.

OMG haha

CHAR

OMGGGG were they cute? Of course they were! [llama heart eye emoji]

Can't tell Abernathy anything, btw. I'm already in my seat across the hall. Like a good student.

E

I'm a good student, too! A good student who is literally running late.

CHAR

Ooh. Extra points for using literally in the correct sense.

E

Told you I'm a good student!

Run, girl. Abernathy's going to lock you out.

E

Just tell her I'll be there in a sneeze! Please! I'll let you borrow my charger at lunch.

I just told you. I can't tell her anything!

I am literally in my own desk across the hall.

(I'm a good student too, Char!)

CHAR

Yes, yes, everyone's a good student.

Pleeeeeease, E, can I borrow your charger anyway?

Also . . . a sneeze? You sound just like my dad.

E

I know! That's what he said when I was looking for you after school.

I was like, a sneeze? What? 😄

Dads. Why?

E

He'll probably stop acting so weird once things settle down.

What things?

E

With the separation and divorce and all that.

My dad was super weird back in the day. But then it all went back to normal.

Well, a new normal. But you know what I mean. It stopped being so weird.

Ok. Almost there! Like flying down the hall so fast my phone wants to dictate my slapping footsteps.

Side note: I've run past like 50 new "check the app" posters. When did those go up?

Newsflash! No one ever needs to check the app!

The relentless fruit cocktail schedule is seared into our brains!

Plus, the app stucks in general.

No, stucks

Stucks

Gah! sucks

But not as much as my phone dictation apparently

CHAR

[eyerolling and laughing emoji]

Wait. How did you know?

E

Know what? About how much the app stucks?

GAH.

There is literally an URGENT fruit cocktail announcement every day, and then, like, two dorks fighting about sweatshirts or basketball practice or who cares.

Omg why is Abernathy such a tyrant? I have to lock up my phone AND I have her two periods in a row! Waaaaah.

No, no, not about the stupid app.

We all know how useless it is.

I'm talking about my parents and the separation.

Mom and Dad said no one knew.

They said they were planning to have coffee with your mom and dad later this week to talk about it, but they wanted to tell me first.

So . . . who told YOU?

E

What do you mean? YOU told me!

Can we talk about this at lunch? I really have to go.

But! Super quick! Inside or outside? For lunch?

I did NOT tell you! The only person I told was Char.

OMG. CHAAAAAR!

CHAR

Uh. Oops?

CHAR!!!!! I SPECIFICALLY ASKED YOU NOT TO SAY ANYTHING!!!

E

OK that is not the answer to my question, and Abernathy is standing here breathing fire, so . . . see you nerds, uh, somewhere at lunch.

Maybe I'll bring my charger, but only if you promise to trade me some fruit cocktail for it. 💀

Hello, ladies, this is Ms. Abernathy. Elena's phone is going into Phone Jail now. I suggest putting your own phones away as well.

CHAR

asdjkhfkjash Ms. Abernathy

Did I do that right?

CHAR!!! YOU TOLD ELENA?????

I TOLD YOU NOT TO

LIKE I SAID OUT LOUD IN MY ACTUAL VOICE

DO

NOT

TELL

ANYONE

AT

ALL

ABOUT

MY

PARENTS

SEPARATING

YOU ARE THE FIRST PERSON IN THE WHOLE WORLD I HAVE TOLD, CHAR!

CHAR

...

CHARRRRRRRRRRRRRRRR

CHAR

...

DO NOT ... ME!

I can't believe you didn't listen to me!

No, worse. I can't believe you didn't HEAR me when I asked you not to say anything.

CHAR

Ava. Whoa. Come on ... the three of us tell each other everything.

When you said not to tell anyone, I didn't think you meant Elena, too!

Elena isn't an anyone. Just like you and I aren't, either.

Best friends aren't anyones, Ava!

Elena, when you rescue your phone from Phone Jail and see this, back me up!

I shouldn't be surprised you didn't listen to me, Char. No one EVER listens to me.

CHAR

WHAT! YOU LITERALLY AREN'T LISTENING TO *ME* RIGHT NOW!

That's a great plan, actually. How about I literally DON'T listen to you for a while?

see how you like it

Battery 39%

NATIONAL NEWS NOW: Llamas evade lasso capture, run amok, baffle authorities. NChopperNow is live above the chaos.

LOCAL NEWS TODAY: Main Street reopens as loose llamas mosey over to Butler Park area.

TEENBUZZ: Show him how strong you are with these new swimsuits that SPARKLE with girl power!

500+ UNREAD LOLMS NOTIFICATIONS

Today 9:06 AM

CHAR

Ava, I'm sorry.

For real.

Today 10:10 AM

CHAR

It's not like I didn't listen, I just . . .

I guess I didn't really understand that "don't tell anyone" actually meant ANYONE.

Plus, I thought E could help.

She's been through it, you know?

Today 10:55 AM

CHAR

feel free to jump in any time here, Elena . . .

HER PHONE IS IN ABERNATHY'S PHONE JAIL, CHAR!

CHAR

Still? How?

BACK-TO-BACK CLASSES! DUH!

SEE??? YOU DON'T LISTEN! NOT EVEN WITH YOUR EYES!

CHAR

I WAS JUST SAYING THAT FOR WHEN SHE GETS HER PHONE BACK, AVA.

JUST BECAUSE YOU'RE A GOOD STUDENT DOESN'T MEAN YOU ALWAYS KNOW EVERYTHING!

Battery 30%

NATIONAL NEWS NOW: Country holds collective breath as two so-called therapy llamas menace small town. Click for LIVE footage.

LOCAL NEWS TODAY: Llamas identified as therapy llamas Bea and Arthur. Owners provide police with ten pounds of peppermint candies to assist in luring llamas out of Butler Park.

TEENBUZZ: It's not YOUR fault your man is mad. OR IS IT? Take this URGENT quiz to find out.

500+ UNREAD LOLMS NOTIFICATIONS

E

Uh-oh.

Yeah, uh-oh.

E

You know how much I hate it when you two get like this.

I don't want to be your referee, I want to be your friend.

I could strangle her!

I COULD STRANGLE YOU, CHARRRRR!

CHAR

I thought E would have better advice than me.

To help you feel better.

I don't like to see you sad.

What if MY help can't help you because I don't know HOW to help?

Seriously. You're making me flip text in incomplete sentences.

And you know how that makes me flip out.

Haha. Get it?

Ava. Come on.

I already said this, but I'll say it again ... there are no secrets between you and me and E.

At least that's what I thought.

E

Just popping in to say I *also* thought that.

Popping out again.

Friends Don't Make Friends Be Their Referee. FDMFBTR.

Today 11:50 AM

E

Uuuggghhhhhhh. Ava. Where you at?

Char, where are YOU?

Is ANYONE going to eat lunch with me today?

Can't we all chat it out over lukewarm green beans?

I'm in the bathroom

E

Well, hurry up. Lunch line is long.

28

The tables outside will be fulllllll before we ever get out there.

Unless Char is already out there saving a table.

I'm not feeling super great.

E

Because you yelled at Char like a texting howler monkey?

I wouldn't feel great about that, either.

Sorry. I'm staying out of it. Neutral. The Switzerland of friends.

Or, wait, was Switzerland actually kind of 😯 *not* neutral?

Like, back in the olden days?

Idk.

I just want to stay here for lunch.

Or maybe GO to Switzerland.

E

Stay in the *bathroom*? That's so gross, Ava.

Are you sick for real? Like, cramps, or something?

Cramps IN MY HEART.

E

Cramps in your heart from what?

From Char telling me about your parents splitting up?

Aw, come on. She was just trying to help. She's worried about you.

Sigh. Maybe you're right.

And now I have EXTRA cramps in my heart because of ALL-CAPSing Char like that.

Mostly the heart cramps are because of my parents, though

How can they just split up like this?

It all feels so fast.

One day Mom's making me breakfast for school, the next day she's signing a lease on an apartment. WHAT?!?

I mean, ALL Mom's clothes are gone, E.

ALL OF THEM.

E

It stinks to be caught off guard. Trust me. I know.

It all gets easier though.

I know you're trying to help, but it also stinks to hear it'll get easier. No offense.

That's kind of why I wanted to wait to tell you.

I don't WANT it to get easier.

I don't WANT to look on the bright side or find any silver linings or whatever.

I want everything to go back to the way it was.

E

Honestly, Ava? It kind of cramps MY heart that you didn't want me to know.

Talk about off guard. Ouch.

And I know this isn't very Switzerland of me to say, but Char's totally right, you know.

Best friends aren't anyones.

Best friends are everything.

E

But fine, I'll stop telling you it'll be ok

Uuuugghhhhhhhh you're right.

I'm sorry I'm acting like such a bag of jerks.

E

I don't think that's a saying.

But even so, I get what YOU'RE saying.

I think.

😡 You're just so good at being positive.

I'm not ready to be positive.

Not yet.

Maybe not even ever.

And I didn't want to make YOU feel bad for not being able to stop ME from feeling bad.

Except now I HAVE made you feel bad. And I've made CHAR feel bad.

EVERYONE feels bad, and it's all my fault because clearly my heart cramps are contagious, so yeah, I'm staying in the gross bathroom for lunch.

Today 12:16 PM

Char?

I'm sorry I got so mad.

I totally see how you were trying to help.

I totally see that I overreacted.

I'm totally sorry for going all ALL CAPS howler monkey on you.

I am ALSO totally sorry for being a heart cramps super spreader.

Though maybe blame that on my parents because they started it.

Come on, Char, forgive me?

Char?

E

It's possible we might have literally blown up her flipper with 124872378524 texts.

Oh man. Lockdown drill? What the heck?

E

Probably from Char's phone blowing up.

You crack yourself up, don't you? 😆 🙄

E

 All the time.

Where are we even supposed to go during a lunchtime drill?

E

There are about 600 new posters in the cafeteria reminding everyone to Check the App for principal updates and assignments and blah blah blah.

Maybe we should actually check the app for once.

Ha

Your jokes aren't as funny when there's a BLARING ALARM annoying me.

I'll be even more annoyed if I have to scroll through a year of unread notifications on the app right now.

E

No one seems to be going anywhere, maybe i'll just stay in line and wait for the all clear.

I don't know, E. Remember last lockdown drill?

E

Ooh. Good point. Who knew you could get in-school suspension for being too slow to duck and cover?

Well, I know NOW.

And THAT terrible lesson is why I'm leaving the bathroom.

It's also why you should leave the lunch line.

E

I don't really want to lose my place in line, though.

And aren't you supposed to just stay in the bathroom during a lockdown drill?

Isn't that, like, the second rule of lockdown or something?

I don't care what rule of lockdown it is.

I am NOT sitting on a toilet tank and putting my feet on the seat. Grosssss.

E

Says the girl who is purposely spending her *lunchtime* in the bathroom. 😖

If I leave the lunch line, where would I even go?

Where are YOU going?

An open classroom, I guess?

OMG THIS ALARM IS SO LOUD

We get it! There's a drill!

E

Do you think they call it a drill because the sound drills into your brain?

You sound like Char. 🎧

OMG WHY HASN'T IT STOPPED YET?

E

Gooood question.

I think I'll just hang out with the lunch ladies for a minute. See what shakes out.

I hope you don't lunch lady yourself into ISS.

E

What does that even mean??

Come find me when the drill is over, ok?

And, Char, wherever you are, come find us, too. Pleeeease.

Pleeeeease, Char! I want to say I'm sorry face-to-face.

And then maybe hug your face, if you'll let me.

And then hug Elena's face, too, for Being Real with Me™ instead of being Switzerland.

Today 12:31 PM

Where am I supposed to go if every classroom door is locked?

E

Everyone in here is kinda freaking out, Ava.

Find a hiding spot, ok?

I don't know if this is a drill or not.

What?

E

Uh

I just saw Ms. Nichols RUNNING past.

"If I see you run, you get lunch detention for the entire rest of your life because LOL students are exemplary and exemplary students never run inside buildings" Ms. Nichols?

E

YES!

Like, full speed RUNNING.

E, where are you?

E

I told you. I'm in the kitchen with the lunch ladies.

Me and Xi and that Towson kid and a couple others.

Hang on.

E??

Char??

Where are you?

CHAR???

Today 12:36 PM

E

Omg

No, I get to omg YOU.

Where did you go??

Have you heard anything from Char?

Like, literally EVERY classroom is locked.

Where am I supposed to go???

Ms. Nichols ran in and turned off the lights.

We're laying on the floor, Ava!

The sticky gross floor behind the lunch buffet!

Lying.

E

I AM NOT LYING.

No, I mean . . . that's what Char said to me this morning. It's lying, not laying.

E

This is no joke, Ava!!

This isn't a drill, maybe you should go back into the bathroom.

I can hear more running out in the hall by the cafeteria.

One of the lunch ladies is crying.

She wants to use my phone.

BRB

Wait. WHAT

DADDIO

Today 12:41 PM

Dad?

DADDIO

This is an autoresponse! Do Not Disturb is activated because I'm driving. When I stop driving, I'll see this message and get back to you. Safety first!

Nooooooooo.

Dad! Text me as soon as you see this.

There's a lockdown at school.

I think it might be real.

I'm kind of freaking out here.

People are yelling down by the library.

All the classrooms are locked.

I don't know where to go.

MAMABEAR

Today 12:42 PM

Mom?

MAMABEAR

This is an autoresponse! Do Not Disturb is activated because I'm driving. When I stop driving, I'll see this message and get back to you. Safety first!

Omgggggggggggg

Why are you and Dad SO CHEESY?

And where is everyone driving in the middle of the day??

Don't you have work???

Text me back!

Some kind of lockdown is happening at school.

E is, like, on the floor in the cafeteria?

I can't find Char!

I can't find a place to hide.

I don't know what to do.

I'm starting to get really scared.

12:45 PM

Battery 20%

NATIONAL NEWS NOW: Could YOUR local authorities safely corral wild animals? LIVE NChopperNow tracks escaped llamas as they rampage through small town.

LOCAL NEWS TODAY: Escaped therapy llamas Bea and Arthur earn spontaneous applause as they dash by nursing facility, ignoring peppermint-laced traps.

TEENBUZZ: He wants to see those muscles! You'll never believe how easy arm workouts can be!

500+ UNREAD LOLMS NOTIFICATIONS

E & CHAR

Today 12:46 PM

Char, where ARE YOU?

I'm not mad anymore.

Please talk to me.

Where are you?

Are you in a safe place?

I can't find a place to hide.

All the classrooms are locked.

Cafeteria is locked.

There's yelling by the library.

NOT going that way.

If you tell me where you are, I can go there

And maybe you can let me in?

Char!

TEXT ME BACK

Elena, do u have your phone back?

If I run to the cafeteria and bang on the door, will you let me in?

E?

TEXT ME BACK!

Omg Diego saved my life

He saw me run by the art room and yelled at me to hide with them.

I guess he and some other kids have been watching out the window in the door and grabbing kids trapped in the hallway.

I told him the window on the door is supposed to be covered.

That's like the second rule of lockdown after locking the door

But he yelled at me.

Like, YELLED at me, Char!

And said he'd never been in a lockdown drill before.

And there are like a million tater tots freaking out in here.

And now they want me to tell them what's going on.

I DON'T KNOW WHAT'S GOING ON

SOMEBODY TEXT ME BACK

AND ALSO BABYD

OOPS SORRY

DIEGO

HAS A MESSAGE FOR CHAR

ALSO SORRY ABOUT SO MANY ALL CAPS BUT IT IS AN ALL CAPS SITUATION RIGHT NOW

Hey, Char, it's Diego.

Do YOU know what's going on?

Ava doesn't know anything.

Also, next time Mom says I can't have a phone please remind her I might get stuck in an art room again one day and Ava won't be there with her phone to save me.

Except Ava's phone has 10% battery.

Also, do u know where my inhaler is?

I thought I had an extra in my backpack but I can't find it

Hi, Char, it's me again.

My phone's about to die.

PLEASE TEXT ME BACK.

Or, if you're mad at me, can you at least text E?

Diego and I just want to make sure you're safe.

Also, Diego just dumped his backpack EVERYWHERE.

He can't find his breathy asthma medicine thing and he's trying to be chill but I can tell he's scared.

He said his chest feels tight.

45

Is there anything else that might help him?

Last summer was SCARY and he seems a little freaked…

And I'm a little freaked at the idea of adding last summer's scary on top of THIS scary.

DADDIO

Today 1:06 PM

DADDIO

It is I, your father!

I just got your texts.

What's up?

Drill over?

> I don't think it's a drill.

> No one knows what's going on.

> I'm hiding in the art room.

DADDIO

What about your teacher?

> There's no teacher in here!

> Just me and a million tater tots.

DADDIO

?

> 6th graders.

DADDIO

Why is there no teacher?

I don't know!

I think the room was empty because it was lunchtime.

Everyone who was in the hall or the bathroom when the alarm went off ended up here.

It's like the Island of Misfit Toys but with tater tots.

And me.

DADDIO

?

THE MOVIE, DAD. WITH THE DENTIST ELF???

DADDIO

???

Everyone's freaking out.

Some of the tater tots are crying and that's freaking ME out.

I'm trying to stay calm, though, because if I freak out, they'll freak out even more.

And if there IS someone out there hunting us all down

Or whatever

that person will hear everyone freaking out

and then they'll find us and

48

DADDIO

Hey hey hey

Kiddo

I need you to take a deep breath for me, ok?

A deep breath??

Right now??

Dad!

That might ACTUALLY kill me!

DADDIO

Why?! What's happening?!

You've obviously never been in a room filled with scared-sweaty tater tots!

DADDIO

Ava!

Not funny!

I'm sorry. You're right.

Is it weird that I seem to joke more when I'm scared?

I'm super scared right now, so prepare yourself.

DADDIO

It's not weird at all, kiddo.

Laughing or joking when you're afraid is a normal psychological reaction for many people.

Some psychologists suggest that it's a kind of denial, others frame it as more of a defense mechanism.

It's always a good idea to make sure people can *tell* you're joking, though.

So that you don't give them a heart attack.

 Dadsplaining alert!

Sorry.

It IS really stinky in here, though.

I had no idea how much scared tater tots could sweat.

DADDIO

Sweating is actually a perfectly normal physiological reaction to stress.

I bet I can find this really interesting study my colleague wrote about it a few years ago.

Have you ever met Dave? I think you did once. Maybe in the office that one time Mom's car wouldn't start

DADDIO is typing . . .

DAD!

You're doing that thing where you get nervous or whatever and you just talk and talk except now it's with texting.

Is overexplaining is a normal parental reaction for many adults under stress?

Maybe you need to take a deep breath, too?

DADDIO

Ah. You're right.

Good observation, kiddo.

Also, good idea.

Let's try to calm down together, ok?

I know that's a hard ask right now, but please, let's both try to stay calm.

Dad. Don't say "hard ask."

DADDIO

Omg did you just use an emoji?

It IS the end of the world.

DADDIO

Slow breath In.

Slow breath out.

Slow breath in.

Slow breath out.

Keep doing that until your shoulders relax.

How did you know my shoulders were tense?

DADDIO

How do dads know anything?

Magic.

Today 1:20 PM

DADDIO

Hey, have you talked to Mom yet?

You should text her and tell her what's going on.

I got her driving autorespond thing

DADDIO

Ok, I'm going to try to get in touch with her really quick.

Ok

DADDIO

I don't know why I'm even asking you this, but . . . watch me dare to dream . . . is your phone charged?

Not really.

DADDIO

Alright. Not a surprise. Do you have a charger?

No.

DADDIO

NOW do you see why I always tell you to keep your phone charged?

Phone charged, charger in backpack, Ava.

PHONE CHARGED, CHARGER IN BACKPACK!

We've been OVER this and over this.

DAD! Don't yell at me right now!

Trust me. I'VE LEARNED MY LESSON!

DADDIO

Deep breaths.

Can you see if anyone else has a charger you can borrow?

I'm going to call Mom.

And I'm going to look for more info on what's happening.

You're doing great.

No I'm not.

DADDIO

You are, kiddo.

You

are

doing

great.

I'm so proud of you.

I love you.

I love you, too, Daddy.

I'm sorry I yelled at you.

You can say "hard ask" any time you want.

Except.

No. Not really.

Because what if hard ask is the last thing
we ever talk about.

DADDIO

Deep breaths.

Deep breaths.

Just stay in the now, ok?

I'm going to go see what I can find out.

E

Ava! Char! Are you two ok?

The lunch lady gave my phone to that kid Towson and he kept it FOREVER!

E! omg.

Are YOU ok?

E

Still alive.

Still on the floor in the cafeteria.

Still wondering where you are.

In the art room

Diego's here, too.

E

Is he ok?

He's mostly fine.

But he needs his asthma medicine breathy thing.

It's not in his backpack.

He's getting kind of freaked out.

And so am I.

E

omg

He's breathing fine, though, right?

Not like last summer?

Is there no teacher with you?

He's breathing fine right now

No, no teacher.

Just me stranded on this Island of Misfit Tater Tots.

Diego IS kind of wide-eyed and freaking, but I think it's just My-First-Lockdown™ freak out.

Not breathing freak out

E

Have the tater tots never had a drill before?

We haven't had one in ages, have we?

Never!

Well, they probably had the elementary school ones.

But those are like "let's hide from the Big Bad Wolf" or whatever.

They're not the same.

And now it's not even a drill!!

No wonder the tater tots are all melting down.

Remember how freaked out Char got in 6th grade when we had our first drill?

E

Not freaked out, Ava.

She was panicked.

It's different.

And, yeah.

I could hear her crying all the way down the hall in the gym.

That was almost scarier than the actual drill.

I hope she's ok right now.

E

Me, too.

Char, where ARE you?

I wish I knew.

Omg my phone is at like 5%.

Maybe there's a charger in here.

I'm going to see if I can find one.

BRB

MAMABEAR

Today 1:42 PM

MAMABEAR

Ava!

I saw your texts

Are you ok?

What's happening now?

You're still in a safe place?

I'm in the art room which I guess is safe?

We're trying to be as quiet as possible so we can hear what's going on out in the hallway.

And so no one out there can hear US.

The only thing I can actually hear, though, is all the tater tots' scared breathing.

Do YOU know what's going on?

MAMABEAR

I'm trying to find out, baby.

Try to stay calm, ok?

Can you hang on? Dad's calling.

I'll be right back.

I love you.

Not Delivered

1:45 PM

Battery 0%

NATIONAL NEWS NOW: Panel of experts weigh in: Llamas' erratic behavior grows more worrisome by the hour.

LOCAL NEWS TODAY: Bea and Arthur enjoy flower snack in highway median as rescue team closes in. THIS IS A DEVELOPING STORY.

TEENBUZZ: Is there such a thing as TOO MUCH muscle mass? If you're a young woman, that answer might be YES.

600+ UNREAD LOLMS NOTIFICATIONS

LOLMS GLOBAL ANNOUNCEMENTS

URGENT

PLEASE, BEFORE YOU COMMENT, READ TO THE END OF THIS POST.

Good afternoon, LOL family. I know this day hasn't progressed in a way any of us would have chosen or planned, but I want you to know that I am incredibly proud of each and every one of you for the calm bravery I expect from an LOL Hurricane. I cannot tell you how the rest of the day will unfold, but I CAN tell you that staying calm, following the lockdown rules you all know so well, and waiting for instructions from your teachers, me, and/or the police, will get us all safely home soon.

Every student should have access to the app through their personal mobile phones, or through their school-issued laptop. However, if there are students in your classroom who do *not* have access to the app for any reason, please relay this information to them and please add their name next to your name in the comments below.

ONLY ADD NAMES OF STUDENTS WHO ARE PHYSICALLY IN THE SAME ROOM WITH YOU.

- Yes, there is an intruder in the school
- We know he does not have access to the app
- The police are outside the school and they are working hard to end this ordeal safely for EVERYONE

- Please DO NOT LEAVE your classroom until a police officer comes to the door and escorts you from the building
- Please make sure all doors are locked and all classroom windows are covered
- Please keep away from all windows and doors
- Never open the door to anyone unless it is a police officer with the codeword: LOL
- Please stay as silent as possible
- Please keep your phones quiet as well
- Please be kind to your teachers and to one another
- Please stay calm

PLEASE CONTINUE TO CHECK THE APP FOR UPDATES.

I AM SO PROUD OF ALL OF YOU,

Principal Nichols

Posted by Principal Nichols today, 1:42 PM

COMMENTS:

Dwayne R: First!

Veronica J: Don't be a LOL HURRICANES, Dwayne.

Dwayne R: YOU'RE a LOL HURRICANES, VERONICA.

Elise M: Whoa. I've never seen a global announcement with comments turned on before.

Veronica J: looks like they turned on a language filter, too.

Dwayne R: You bet your LOL HURRICANES they did. Those LOL HURRICANES aren't LOL HURRICANES.

Veronica J: Veronica Johnson, Room 222. Where is Ms. Nichols?

Ms. Nichols? Are you monitoring the comments?

Peter M: Peter Morrison, Room 425. Hey, Sean, where are you?

Aarush B: Sean P or Sean H? I saw Sean P walking to lunch earlier.

Sean H: I'm Sean H! I'm in the band hall.

Katy P: Katy Perez here, has anyone seen Towson? We got separated at the beginning of the drill.

Dwayne R: It's not a drill, LOL HURRICANES. Did you even read the LOL HURRICANES message from Nichols?

Veronica J: SHUT UP, DWAYNE! You're not a LOL HURRICANES, Katy.

Dwayne R: I'm just kidding, jeez.

Jung K: Can someone stuff Dwayne in a closet?

Dwayne R: Joke's on you, Jung. I'm already IN a closet.

Veronica J: Can everyone just STOP for a second and let people check in like Ms. Nichols asked.

Hena K: Speaking of, why is Veronica policing the LOL HURRICANES here and not Ms. N?

Aarush B: Why would Veronica be policing Ms. N?

Hena K: No, Aarush, that's not what I meant.

Jung K: I think you just dangled your modifier?

Dwayne R: That's what she said.

Dwayne R: Oh, score! That's what she saids aren't censored!

Veronica J: SHUT UPPPPPPPPPP, DWAYNEEEEEEEEEE, BEFORE I LOL HURRICANES YOU!

Carl Y: Maybe Ms. Nichols is busy ninja-fighting the intruder guy?

Carl Y: Maybe she's crawling through the AC ducts so she can surprise attack the intruder guy!

Carl Y: Ooh! TWIST! Maybe she IS the intruder guy!

Veronica J: Ok, now it's time for YOU to shut up, Carl.

Hena K: I just looked in the app settings. Someone turned off commenting for admin users, but turned it on for student users.

Dwayne R: Ooh, can that same someone turn off the language filter, too?

Elise M: Why would that even be an option??

Dwayne R: Sometimes swearing is *good* for you, Hena!

Elise M: That's not what I meant, Dwayne! I meant why would the app let admin be locked out of a post, but not students?

Hena K: Who knows. The app is so LOL HURRICANES.

Billy S: Billy Sanchez, Abernathy's room.

Sean P: I'm here! Hey, Peter and Aarush. You guys ok?

Aarush B: Sean! Finally! Where were you, dude?

Sean P: Bowers made us lock our phones into those LOL HURRICANES pouches.

Sean P: Wait. Why can't I say LOL HURRICANES?

Sean P: Seriously?? LOL HURRICANES isn't even a bad word!!

Sean P: Anyway, it took forever to get all our LOL HURRICANES phones out of those LOL HURRICANES pouches.

Jung K: Is anyone else, like, scared right now? Why are you all acting so normal?

Veronica J: NO ONE IS ACTING NORMAL, JUNG! EVERYONE IS SCARED!

Jung K: Ok, ok, you don't have to yell at me.

Veronica J: Sorry.

Aarush B: You can't really see crying in comments.

Several people are typing . . .

MAMABEAR

Today 1:50 PM

MAMABEAR

Ava?

Everything still ok?

Ava!

I don't know what's going or if you can see this, but if you can, I want you to know I'm here.

Well, I'm parked as close to school as I can get.

I can't come and get you because the police are setting up a barricade and they won't let anyone past.

But as soon as I can storm the school, I'm in.

I'll haul you out just like Kevin Costner saved Whitney in The Bodyguard.

Ava?

Are you getting these texts?

I'm thinking maybe not if the bad movie joke didn't get a response.

Ava baby, I love you.

I'm right here.

2:00 PM

Battery 10%

NATIONAL NEWS NOW: Police activating llama SWAT at last? Authorities descend on middle school as llamas continue to evade capture. THIS IS A DEVELOPING STORY.

LOCAL NEWS TODAY: Unconfirmed reports of large police presence at Lila O'Lowry Middle School. THIS IS A DEVELOPING STORY.

MISSED CALL MAMABEAR

MISSED CALL DADDIO

MISSED CALL MAMABEAR

MISSED CALL MAMABEAR

2+ MISSED CALLS

700+ UNREAD LOLMS NOTIFICATIONS

Did I miss anything?

E

You missed me growing a beard while I waited for your phone to charge!

Did that take a thousand years?

It feels like that took a thousand years.

Uuuuggghhhhh. Sorry.

It's only the first thousand years of a million more, too.

This tater tot's charger is a SOLAR charger.

I had to tear a little corner of paper off the window to get it to work.

But not enough paper so that some wannabe poser intruder dingdong can see inside.

So, not only does this charger ALREADY suck, it's extraaaaa slow.

My phone is already about to die again.

E

SOLAR charger? Why?

Who knows?

He's a tater tot.

Why do they do anything?

Have you heard anything from Char?

Diego really needs his asthma breather thingy

and I know she can't just run over here with one

but maybe she knows some tricks for keeping him calm and breathing easy?

Like the ones Moppa had him do last summer when the ambulance took forever?

MAMABEAR

Ava?

I need you to check in as soon as you safely can, ok?

> Hi! Sorry! My phone died and I had to borrow a charger from a tater tot, but for some dumb reason it's a solar charger and it's soooooo slooooooow.

MAMABEAR

DO NOT EVER DO THAT TO ME AGAIN.

I AM TRYING TO STAY CALM BUT YOU JUST DISAPPEARED.

IN THE MIDDLE OF . . . WHATEVER THIS THING IS THAT'S HAPPENING.

AND IT IS NOT THAT POOR 6TH GRADER'S FAULT THAT YOU NEVER KEEP YOUR PHONE CHARGED

HOLD ON.

I'M ADDING DAD SO HE CAN TEXT YOU IN ALL CAPS, TOO.

MAMABEAR added DADDIO

DADDIO

AVA! THANK GOD!

DON'T JUST DISAPPEAR LIKE THAT!

Sorry. 😡

I'm doing a lot of stuff right now!

Tater tots are flipping out everywhere.

And all phones have to be silenced, so I don't always know when I have a new text.

Also, pleeeease stop trying to call.

No phone calls allowed.

That's like the second rule of lockdown, you guys.

MAMABEAR

Right. Of course. I guess I *do* know that.

I vaguely remember some of the rules from the lockdown slideshow at the PTA meeting ages ago.

It's just . . .

It's hard to follow rules when we don't know what's going on, Ava.

You understand that, right?

YES! I hate the rules, too, Mom!

But I don't know what's going on either!

And *I'm* still trying to do all the things they told us would keep us safe.

Or not do them.

Or whatever!

You know what I mean!

DADDIO

You're doing a great job, kiddo.

We'll work on doing better, too.

We just want to know you're ok.

We want everyone to be ok.

I'm ok.

Elena is in the cafeteria and she's still ok.

Char is mad and won't answer my texts, so I hope she's ok.

Diego could really use his asthma breather thingy, but other than that, he's like 93% ok.

Do you know any of those breathing exercise he was doing with Moppa last summer?

He asked if I could breathe with him, but I don't really know what that means.

I wish there was a way everyone in the school could text each other. Maybe another kid has a locker close by with an inhaler in it.

Heck, maybe someone actually knows what's going on.

MAMABEAR

Let me call Jo and ask about the breathing exercises. She doesn't usually answer when she's at work, though. She might not even know what's going on!

JB, can you call Thea?

DADDIO

Already on it!

Ava, try slow deep breaths with Diego.

Keeping him calm certainly can't hurt.

I know asthma is a physiological condition, but sometimes you can affect your physiology with psychological exercises.

MAMABEAR

JB. You're doing that thing you do.

DADDIO

Right.

Sorry.

Dadsplaining is my crutch when I feel the need to dissipate spiraling emotions.

MAMABEAR

And there we go again. 😉

DADDIO

Deep breaths.

For everyone.

MAMABEAR

Ava?

DADDIO

Hello?

MAMABEAR

She's gone again

DADDIO

Indeed

She seems pretty calm though, considering.

MAMABEAR

Calmer than I am, that's for sure.

DADDIO

Where are you? Do you want me to find you?

MAMABEAR

I'm at the barricade.

The press are all showing up now.

It's a circus.

No one will tell us anything.

DADDIO

I'll be there in five.

E

Ava? This is Ms. Nichols on Elena's phone.

Elena says there's a student with you having an asthma attack?

Yes, Ms. Nichols.

He's mostly ok right now.

But he's definitely getting kind of worse.

So, yeah, it's like a pre-attack, I guess?

E

What's his name?

Diego.

He's my friend Charlotte's brother.

He's a tater tot.

I mean 6th grader.

E

Are YOU ok, Ava?

No!

I mean not really.

I'm scared but I'm not screaming crying puking scared.

At least not yet.

Is there really someone here trying to hurt us?

THAT might make me screaming crying puking scared.

E

You're in the safest place you can be right now, ok?

I might be, but Diego isn't.

He really needs his asthma medicine breather thing.

E

Inhaler.

Inhaler.

Diego needs one, like, now

E

Can you tell me what color his lips are?

MAMABEAR & DADDIO
Today 2:27 PM

DADDIO

Ava? You there?

Mom and I are together now

MAMABEAR

Together in PERSON.

Dad means we're *at the barricade* together.

DADDIO

Right.

Sorry if that was confusing.

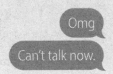

DADDIO

AVA? What do you mean can't talk now?

MAMABEAR

Ava, baby, are you ok?

Sorry, Ms. Nichols.

My parents are trying hard to be extra calm but really they're just being extra.

Diego's lips are regular lip color.

Not blue or anything scary like that.

E

You've seen his lips turn blue before?

Last summer.

Our families always go on vacation to the lake and he had an asthma attack out of nowhere.

His inhaler was in the car.

But the car wasn't there.

We had to call 911.

It's an easier story to tell out loud than with texts.

Elena was there, too. She can tell you all about it.

E

So you know what emergency signs to look for?

Kind of?

I mean, I know it's bad if he's blue.

Or if he's breathing so hard he can't talk.

He won't STOP talking right now.

So, that seems like a good sign.

Except for the part where I might strangle him for talking so much.

E

Do you think you can get him to calm down and take slow easy breaths?

MAMABEAR

Ava? All good over there?

DADDIO

Diego still talking a lot?

I'M IN THE MIDDLE OF SOMETHING!

I'LL BRB!

E

Ava? Do you think you can calm down?

HOW AM I SUPPOSED TO CALM DOWN WHEN WE'RE LOCKED IN A CLASSROOM TRYING TO HIDE FROM . . .

I DON'T EVEN KNOW . . .

AND I'M STUCK ON THE ISLAND OF MISFIT TATER TOTS AND THEY'RE ALL EITHER CRYING OR ACTING LIKE TURDS.

OR, LIKE, HAVING AN ASTHMA ATTACK.

AND MY PARENTS KEEP TEXTING ME AND SAYING THINGS LIKE THEY'RE BACK TOGETHER.

WHICH IS NOT ACTUALLY WHAT THEY'RE SAYING.

AND WHAT IF I NEVER SEE THEM AGAIN?

WHAT IF I NEVER GET TO TELL CHAR I'M SORRY?

E

*Him

Do you think you can calm *him down.

That's what I meant to text.

I'm not as good or fast at this as You Kids These Days.

But now I'm going to need YOU to take some deep breaths, too.

Ok?

Omg.

I forgot you were Ms. Nichols.

Oooops.

Omg, omg.

E

It's ok. I know this is scary and stressful.

I really appreciate everything you're doing right now.

If you stay calm, you can help me help you keep Diego calm.

Please?

I mean, I can try?

But this is, like, the least calming day in the history of time.

FYI.

E

Point taken.

I guess I could get him to talk about comics.

Instead of his current favorite freak out:

What happens if we all get murdered or whatever.

He loves Ms. Marvel.

E

Ok, great idea!

Talk about comics.

Watch his breathing.

Text Elena if his breathing gets so fast he can't talk, or if his lips turn blue.

I'll see if it's possible to get him an inhaler.

You're in the art room, right?

Right.

Thank you, Ms. Nichols.

E

Thank YOU, Ava.

You're doing an amazing job.

I'll be back in touch soon.

Don't go anywhere.

And can you ask everyone in there to please check the App and comment on my update?

Wait. There's an update???

Like, in the app for real?

It's not about fruit cocktail, is it?

Because if it is, fruit cocktail seems a little off topic right now, no offense.

E

I . . . don't know how to respond to that, Ava.

It's an update on the current situation.

And I need everyone to comment so I can have a headcount.

I have to go, ok? You're doing great!

I'm going to figure out how to get an inhaler to Diego.

Hang tight.

Wait! Before you go . . .

What IS going on Ms. Nichols? Like, for real?

E

Stay calm and check the app, Ava.

I promise it's useful for more than just fruit cocktail updates.

At least it is today.

MAMABEAR & DADDIO

Today 2:43 PM

MAMABEAR

AVA MARIE MCDANIELS YOU TEXT ME BACK RIGHT THIS INSTANT

You said you'd BRB and you did not BRB.

Mom, that's not how BRB works.

DADDIO

Tone, Ava.

DAD.

DADDIO

Listen, we're all scared. And I know you're juggling a lot right now. We just want you to keep in touch, ok?

MAMABEAR

Maybe send a quick "hi" every few minutes? It can be like an Ava beacon.

A beacon?

MAMABEAR

Yeah!

Like an airplane blip on a flight controller's radar.

Or the flash of a light on a lighthouse.

Or the ping your phone makes when you lose it and activate Find My Phone.

I need regular Find My Ava blips, flashes, and pings, ok?

DADDIO

Fun fact! When someone says "Ping me" it's a reference to the ping noise a submarine beacon makes.

Dad.

MAMABEAR

JB.

I reallllllly have to go right now.

Diego needs an inhaler.

And everything is kind of bonkers.

I'll beacon ping you when I can.

DADDIO

Be safe, Ava.

MAMABEAR

We love you!

Be back in a sneeze.

E

Hey, it's E. Got my phone back.

How's Diego?

Could be better.

E

How are you?

Could be better

How are you?

Have you heard from Char?

Do you think she BLOCKED me?

But then why hasn't she texted YOU?

Omg you don't think?

E

NO!!

Nothing has happened.

She probably just turned her phone off. You know how she gets sometimes.

I wish there was a way to find out what's going on in the rest of the school.

Like some kind of gigantic group chat or something.

E

Girl. Ms. Nichols just told you to check the app for updates! Did you already forget?? 😬

THERE IS A LOT GOING ON IN MY BRAIN RIGHT NOW!

And, yes, I totally forgot.

Aarrrgghhhhh!

My battery's already down to 2%.

Stupid solar charger, it doesn't work unless my phone is riiiight up against the little uncovered spot on the window.

And I'm NOT standing next to the window to watch it charge 1% every 1000 years.

E

Uh, yeah. Do NOT stand by the window, Ava!

That's like the second rule of lockdown.

Can you imagine literally dying to find out your phone only has a 3% charge??

Omg

E

Right??

Omg

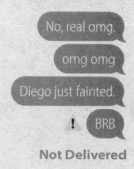

No, real omg.

omg omg

Diego just fainted.

! BRB

Not Delivered

E

AVA!

Get someone ELSE'S PHONE AND TEXT ME BACK.

Except if your phone is dead you can't see this.

Ms. N says not to move!

She's coming to you

MAMABEAR & DADDIO

Today 2:54 PM

MAMABEAR

Who's ready for an Ava ping? THIS MOM.

How's Diego?

Today 2:58 PM

MAMABEAR

Any flashing beacons of hope out there?

Today 3:01 PM

MAMABEAR

Really needing a Hi right now, Ava!

Ava?

Battery 0%

TEENBUZZ: Will wrinkles be extinct before you are? New stem cell study says maybe!

700+ UNREAD LOLMS NOTIFICATIONS

LOLMS GLOBAL ANNOUNCEMENTS

Kevin L: Omg you guys I just saw a kid run past.

Billy S: Your supposed to have your window covered.

Katie McN: You'RE supposed to have YOUR window covered.

Katy P: You GUYS.

Katy P: Who was that in the hallway?

Katie McN: Yeah, who was that????

Jodi E: Jodi E, ELA 7. I think that's room 419?

Jodi E: Also . . . a kid just ran past our classroom. I think . . . it might have been Ava?

Veronica J: Are you in the same class with Kevin L?

Jodi E: Yah.

Veronica J: Did you see 8th grade Ava or 7th grade Ava?

Li X: Or 6th grade Ava?

Billy S: There are three 6th grade Avas.

Tom C: Omg which AVA???

Elise M: The smart one.

Jodi E: The tall one.

Sean P: The one with the short hair.

Elise M: You know AVA Ava.

Dwayne R: Wait AVA Ava is the intruder?

Aaliyah F: Omg

Jodi E: Omg

Tom C: LOL HURRICANES

Veronica J: But the post says the bad guy doesn't have access to the app.

Darryl N: What post?

Veronica J: The post we're all commenting on, LOL HURRICANES!

Veronica J: Seriously??? LOL HURRICANES isn't a bad word at all!

Aarush B: Maybe Ava doesn't have a phone!

Veronica J: Plus, the post says bad GUY.

Aarush B: WHAT ARE AVA'S PRONOUNS????

Elise M: I just saw her run past my class now!

Veronica J: Omg, Elise, GET AWAY FROM THE LOL HURRICANES WINDOW.

Li X: Yeah! Duck and cover, Elise!

Elise M: I know. Sorry. But I wanted to see if it's really her.

Veronica J: And?

Elise M: It's really her!

Darryl N: I just saw her run past, too!

Veronica J: LOL HURRICANES

Veronica J: Where?

Aarush B: Where?

Tom C: Where?

Annemarie H: Where?

Marcela B: Where?

Katie McN: Where?

Darryl N: By the library.

Katy P: I JUST SAW her, too.

Darryl N: Where?

Katy P: In the hall by the gym.

Darryl N: IDK

Dwayne R: Can't be. Gym is too far from the library.

Billy S: Oh, LOL HURRICANES. Maybe there's more than one bad guy.

Elise M: Wait. IS Ava the bad guy?

Katie McN: Why else is she running through the halls?

Hunter J: Hunter Johnson, 7th grade, Room 201.

Dwayne R: Omg, Hunter, we're way past introductions now.

3:20 PM

Charging 1%

LOCAL NEWS TODAY: Police refuse to comment on reports that Lila O'Lowry Middle School is on lockdown. THIS IS A DEVELOPING STORY.

900+ UNREAD LOLMS NOTIFICATIONS

LOLMS GLOBAL ANNOUNCEMENTS

Hunter J: I heard that one time Ava punched her locker because she got a B in gym.

Billy S: I heard that one time Ava screamed for no reason.

Dwayne R: In class?

Li X: Where?

Billy S: IDK . . . just screaming somewhere! IDK. I HEARD it from someone.

Veronica J: Well I KNOW Ava and she's not a LOL HURRICANES locker puncher.

Elise M: I know Ava, too, or kind of do. One time, she let me take the last piece of pizza even though she was in front of me in line.

Dwayne R: Maybe she's lactose intolerant.

Veronica J: OR MAYBE SHE'S JUST A NICE LOL HURRICANES PERSON, DWAYNE.

Dwayne R: WHY WOULD A NICE LOL HURRICANES PERSON DO THIS TO US, VERONICA???

Veronica J: It's more likely she's trying to SAVE us!

Dwayne R: Save us? How?

Jung K: Idk exactly how right now, but she's totally the kind of person who saves people in little ways all the time, you know?

Aarush B: She told me she liked my shoes after Dwayne said something mean.

Dwayne R: What?? LOL HURRICANES, Aarush! I'm not mean! I'm funny! Only a LOL HURRICANES like you can't tell the difference.

Veronica J: AARUSH IS NOT A LOL HURRICANES, DWAYNE!

Aarush B: See? That's like something Ava would do. Thank you, Veronica.

Veronica J: No problem, Aarush.

Hunter J: Omg a shadow went past!!

Jodi E: A shadow?

Hunter J: We have the window covered.

Veronica J: Was it an Ava shaped shadow?

Dwayne R: Or was it a LOL HURRICANES shaped shadow?

Veronica J: SHUT UP, DWAYNE!

Hunter: Why is Ava doing this?

Billy S: I never thought I'd want to go to math, but I want to go to math.

Elise M: I want this to be over.

Billy S: Me too.

Aarush B: Me too.

Hunter J: Me too.

Katy P: Me too.

Jodi E: Me too.

Tom C: Me too.

Katie McN: Me too.

Davy F: Me too.

Carl Y: Me too.

Jung K: Me too.

Aaliyah F: Me too.

Hena K: Me too.

Sean P: Me too.

Marcela B: Me too.

Li X: Me too.

Dwayne R: Well how do we stop her, then?

Billy S: I bet Charles Murphy could stop her. He went to state in wrestling last year.

Tom C: Dude, going to state in wrestling is cool but don't bring a knife to a gunfight.

Billy S: LOL HURRICANES! THERE'S A GUN FIGHT?????

Billy S: I don't want to die.

Hunter J: Me neither.

Charles M: ME NEITHER!!!!!

Billy S: I want to see the ocean before I die.

Elise M: That sounds nice. I want to see the ocean, too. And big snowy mountains.

Dwayne R: I want to have my own comedy special before I die.

Tom C: I want to live all by myself before I die. No parents. No sisters. Just me. And maybe a cat.

Hena K: I want to drive a car before I die.

Veronica J: So do I.

Sean P: I want to be really, really old and ready to die before I die.

Veronica J: So do I.

Aarush B: I want to kiss a girl before I die.

Veronica J: So do I.

Dwayne R: Why would Ava want to hurt any of us???

Veronica J: I TOLD YOU AVA WOULD NEVER DO SOMETHING LIKE THAT.

Dwayne R: But how do you know, Veronica?

Dwayne R: Haven't you ever watched the news?

Dwayne R: Sometimes kids just snap or whatever.

Billy S: That's why my mom won't let me play first person shooter games.

Elise M: Omg, Billy, first person shooter games don't make kids shoot up schools!

Billy S: YOU DON'T KNOW.

Hunter J: I thought school shooters were the kids that get bullied.

Tom C: THAT DOESN'T MAKE ANY SENSE.

Li X: Aren't the BULLIES the ones who want to kill people?

Elise M: NO! Bullies have low self-esteem. That's what Coach Carraway says.

Billy S: WHO BULLIES AVA? THIS IS ALL YOUR LOL HURRICANES FAULT!

Veronica J: Dwayne does.

Dwayne R: I do not!

Veronica J: You do!

Dwayne R: I just tease her.

Dwayne R: That's different.

Veronica J: Is it?

3:35 PM

Battery 3%

NATIONAL NEWS NOW: Unconfirmed reports: Escaped llamas wreak havoc on highway. Police maintain position at middle school, baffling NNN wild animal experts.

1000+ UNREAD LOLMS NOTIFICATIONS

LOLMS GLOBAL ANNOUNCEMENTS

Elena K: EVERYONE!!!

Elena K: SHUT UUUURRRRRPPPPPPPPPPP!!!!

Elena K: LISTEN TO ME I HAVE FACTS.

Elena K: Ava McDaniels is not a bad guy.

Elena K: I don't know what else is going on, but I do know that.

Elena K: REPEAT: AVA MCDANIELS IS NOT A BAD GUY.

Elena K: Also Principal Nichols told me to tell everyone that when she finds out who got into the app settings and set teacher commenting to OFF, they're in big, big, big LOL HURRICANES trouble.

Elena K: Tater tot Diego is having an asthma attack and I'm pretty sure Ava is running around in the halls trying to find him an inhaler.

Gabriel F: I have an inhaler in my backpack right now even though it's supposed to stay in the nurse's office. My mom says it's INSANE to not have it close by.

Veronica J: You can't say insane, Gabriel, that's not nice.

Veronica J: Say, like, wild or idk.

Gabriel: Bonkers?

Veronica J: That's a good one!

Gabriel F: I can slide my inhaler under the classroom door.

Veronica J: Ava, can you see this? Run by room 208!

Elise M: LOL HURRICANES!

Billy S: Did you hear that bang?????

Aarush B: Get away from the windows!!!

Sorry I disappeared!

Diego fainted!

And his face turned a weird color!

I can't even describe it.

Like matte-colored Diego instead of regular-shiny Diego.

And I freaked out.

My phone charged three more percent before I grabbed it and ran.

And now I'm in the hallway running to the nurse's office.

And HOLY 💀 I found an inhaler on the ground in the hall like it's my lucky day or something!

But then, because it is THE WORST UNLUCKIEST DAY EVER, I found it by STEPPING on it and sliding straight into a locker, WHAM.

And there's a SWEATY GUY OUT HERE SOMEWHERE.

I can smell his stink. And I can hear his shouts echoing off the lockers.

Is he screaming MY NAME, E???

CHAR???

IS HE LOOKING FOR ME??? WHY WOULD HE BE LOOKING FOR ME???

E

Omg. Are you ok?

NOOOOOOOOOOOOOOOOOOO

And worse, I crushed the plastic part of the inhaler when I stepped on it.

So THAT'S definitely not ok.

Omg, omg E.

Char.

Someone's running toward me.

Omg.

I don't want to die.

ESPECIALLY in the stinky hallway.

E

You're not going to die, Ava.

You're like the bravest person I've ever known.

Even brave people should hide, though.

Where can you hide?

I don't know.

Idk, idk, idk.

Ok here.

Janitor's closet.

I'm breathing so hard they can probably hear me in space.

My battery's at 2%, so i'm gonna stop texting for a bit, ok?

Love you.

E

Love you, too.

You got this.

Elena K: Well, I have good news and I have bad news.

Aarush B: Good news first!

Elena K: Ava found the inhaler that Gabriel slid under the door.

Elise M: Yay!

Billy S: Woo-hoo.

Veronica J: Awesome.

Gabriel F: Yaaaayyyyyy!

Billy S: Bad news?

Elena K: Bad news is that she found it by stepping on it and crushing it.

Veronica J: LOL HURRICANES

Elena K: Good news!

Aarush B: More good news?

Elena K: That loud bang was Ava sliding into a locker after she tripped on the inhaler.

Dwayne R: Hahaha

Elena K: NOT FUNNY, DWAYNE!

Dwayne R: Sorry.

Dwayne R: And how is that good news?

Elena K: Well, it wasn't a gunshot!

Dwayne R: Ah. Ok. Right. Good news!

Veronica J: But . . . now what. Does the inhaler work?

Elena K: I don't think so.

Aarush B: Where is she?

Elena K: She was in the stinky hallway when she texted me.

Veronica J: AVA, CAN U SEE THIS? GO TO THE BAND ROOM INSTEAD OF THE NURSE.

Veronica J: There are like 53785285769745 inhalers in the band room.

Veronica J: Check all the uniform pockets!

Elena K: Her phone battery's about to die, so I don't think she is looking at the app.

Elise M: What kind of phone does she have? Is she near Mr. Escott's room?

Elise M: I have one of those cases that's a charger . . . I can slide it under the door for her.

Elise M: But she better not step on it.

Elise M: My mom will be super mad.

Elena K: Let me see if she has any juice left.

Elena K: HOLD PLEASE.

Jodi E: Hey all of you everyones? I just totally saw a GUY run past. Right now.

Dwayne R: What do you mean a guy?

Jodi E: Like, not a teacher. A sweaty guy.

Dwayne R: Are you sure it wasn't Ava?

Jodi E: A thousand percent sure.

Veronica J: Where?

Elise M: Where?

Tom C: Where?

Li X: Where?

Hunter J: Where?

Aarush B: Where?

Hena K: Where?

Jodi E: I'm in ELA7 over by the stinky hallway.

Jodi E: I think he might have been shouting AVA actually.

Li X: Omg

Elise M: Omg

Veronica J: LOL HURRICANES!

Tom C: What?

Hunter J: No

Aarush B: Why?

Veronica J: Omg you guys Ava is IN the LOL HURRICANES stinky hallway!!

3:55 PM

🔋

Battery 2%

LOCAL NEWS TODAY: Police are still not commenting on lockdown at LOLMS. THIS IS A DEVELOPING STORY.

1100+ UNREAD LOLMS NOTIFICATIONS

E

Ava! Idk if you're going to see this, but Elise is in Mr. Escott's class and she's going to slide a phone charger case under the door for you. For when you can get over there.

DON'T STEP ON IT!

LOLMS GLOBAL ANNOUNCEMENTS

Marcela B: Omg is the intruder guy really shouting Ava's name?

Aaliyah F: LOL HURRICANES.

Elise M: Omg.

Billy S: What if he sees her?

Aaliyah F: What if he follows her?

Elise M: Who even is he?

Billy S: Why is he doing this?

Dwayne R: Does he know her??

Hena K: How could he KNOW her?

Aarush B: I hate this.

Billy S: HE JUST WALKED PAST OUR LOL HURRICANES CLASS!

Billy S: We heard his feet.

Dwayne R: How do you know it was him?

Elise M: Omg shut up it was him.

Elise M: Who else is out there?

Aarush B: AVA IS OUT THERE.

Veronica J: WELL IT WASN'T HER.

Dwayne R: HOW DO YOU KNOW, VERONICA.

Veronica J: I JUST DO, DWAYNE.

Li X: Which way?

Aarush B: Which way?

Elise M: Where are you?

Hunter J: Where?

Hena K: Where?

Billy S: I'm in Ms. Abernathy's room.

Veronica J: Noooooooooooo.

Billy S: I am there, though. That's totally where I am.

Veronica J: No I mean nooooooo because Abernathy is CLOSER to the LOL HURRICANES nurse's office.

Billy S: Oh.

Billy S: Right.

Hunter J: Maybe Ava heard his sweaty feet and went a different way.

Li X: Or maybe she can somehow check the app and can see everything we're saying.

Aarush B: BE SAFE, AVA.

Elise M: YOU CAN DO IT, AVA.

Billy S: We can hear him outside our room omg.

Billy S: HE'S TOTALLY SHOUTING AVA, AVA, AVA, I JUST WANT TO TALK.

Billy S: I'm so scared, omg.

Elise M: Its ok, Billy.

Veronica J: Stay calm, Billy.

Veronica J: Billy?

Aarush B: You ok?

Dwayne R: Billy?

Billy S: You guys you guys he's not shouting AVA he's shouting ADA!

Dwayne R: How do you know?

Hena K: How can you tell?

Billy S: Because Abernathy just started crying.

Billy S: She told us her name is ADA.

Billy S: LOL HURRICANES
Billy S: LOL HURRICANES
Billy S: LOL HURRICANES
Billy S: The bad guy is looking for HER! For Abernathy!

3:57 PM

Battery 0%

NATIONAL NEWS NOW: Unconfirmed reports: Lila O'Lowry Middle School lockdown is connected to unnamed teacher in the building, not escaped and potentially dangerous llamas.

1300+ UNREAD LOLMS NOTIFICATIONS

E & CHAR

Today 3:58 PM

CHAR

E! Ava is here!

E

Here where????????

And omg WHERE HAVE YOU BEEN?

CHAR

Nurse's office

And . . .

Nurse's office

E

Why have you been radio silent this whole time????

OMG, CHAR, WE WERE SUPER WORRIED!

LIKE STOMACHACHE WORRIED, CHAR!

CHAR

Sorry, sorry.

Ava was so mad, and all these emotions started spiraling up in my chest.

I could feel the panic attack about to crash in on me, and Nurse Shirley is really good at calming me down when I'm panicking.

I came to see her, just like we agreed I would do after the last time. But then, all this [waves arms] started happening and I got stuck here.

WOW am I glad to see Ava!!!

Nurse Shirley is po'd though.

WHY WERE YOU IN THE HALLS?!

DO YOU KNOW HOW DANGEROUS THAT IS?????????

Stuff like that.

Ava told us everything though and omg she HAS to get back to Diego, E.

E

I know, I know! Did she get the inhaler?

CHAR

Yeah, but Nurse Shirley doesn't want her to leave.

And Ava's phone is dead.

Obviously

because Ava's phone is ALWAYS dead [eye roll emoji]

E

Tell her that Elise slid a phone charger under Mr. Escott's door.

It should be in the hallway by the gym.

If Ava can get there without being seen by the intruder guy

who is apparently NOT shouting Ava's name.

He's trying to find Ms. Abernathy, whose name is ADA!

CHAR

WHAT

E

I KNOW

CHAR

Omg, omg who IS this guy?

It's so scary, E.

I just want to go home.

E

Me, too.

CHAR

What if we . . .

What if Diego . . .

E

No, no, no, no.

CHAR

But what if????

E

We'll deal with that IF it happens.

But it won't.

CHAR

How do you know?

E

I don't.

CHAR

Omg Ava just promised Nurse Shirley that she wouldn't leave

AND THEN SHE LEFT

[laughing skull emoji] asgsjhfgalf

On second thought . . . a laughing skull seems like maybe not the best fake emoji to use right now.

E

Nothing is the best of anything right now.

CHAR

Should I follow Ava?

Am I the worst sister ever?

For staying here when my brother needs help?

I just

I don't run fast!

And I scream a lot.

And I am not a ninja

Or a superhero

Or a combination of the two like Ava.

E

It's ok, Char

It's ok.

You're a great sister and a great friend.

CHAR

You're a great friend, too, E.

And Ava's a great friend, too.

She's terrible at keeping her phone charged

And sometimes she gets mad without thinking

But she IS a good friend

E

Yeah.

CHAR

And she's out there trying to save my brother's life.

E

Yeah.

CHAR

Diego's going to be ok, right?

And Ava, too?

E

Totally.

Hey, can you hang on a second?

I'm getting like 32868587245 notifications from the app

BRB

Hunter J: Why does the intruder guy keep screaming ADA, ADA, ADA like that??

Elise M: It's so scary.

Billy S: He sounds so mad.

Billy S: Abernathy looks so scared.

Billy S: Like, she's trying not to be

Billy S: But she's shaking so much her HAIR is vibrating.

Aarush B: Omg

Veronica J: Omg

Billy S: She might even be more scared than I am and this is the most LOL HURRICANES scared I've ever been.

Veronica J: Should we try to get her out of there?

Hena K: Out of where?

Dwayne R: The classroom?

Aarush B: Where would she go?

Dwayne R: That's a LOL HURRICANES idea!!

Veronica J: But he just walked PAST Abernathy's room . . .

Dwayne R: So?

Veronica J: So maybe he doesn't know which classroom is hers?

Veronica J: She could sneak out and make a run for it.

Dwayne R: She should stay put.

Dwayne R: That's like the second rule of lockdown!

Veronica J: I KNOW, DWAYNE. WE ALL KNOW THAT. LOL HURRICANES.

Dwayne R: THE LOL HURRICANES TATER TOTS DON'T KNOW THAT, VERONICA.

Aarush B: I can't believe I'm saying this, but Dwayne is right? She shouldn't try to run away.

Veronica J: If the screamy guy doesn't know where she is, he's going to look everywhere.

Dwayne R: THAT'S NOT A GOOD THING!

Veronica J: But it kind of is because maybe we can trick him.

Aaliyah F: Trick him how?

Aarush B: We have to be SILENT!

Li X: That's like the second rule of lockdown.

Veronica J: I KNOW, but hear me out . . .

Veronica J: If we can make a loud noise on the opposite side of the school from Abernathy's room

Veronica J: Or, idk, distract him somehow, so that he goes that way, then maybe she can escape.

Veronica J: Or at least he'll be further away from her.

Dwayne R: Farther.

Veronica J: SHUT UP, DWAYNE.

Billy S: Ok well Abernathy is reading this over my shoulder.

Billy S: She says not to do any of this.

Billy S: She says to stay as quiet as possible.

Billy S: She says she's so sorry she's already put us all in this much danger.

Veronica J: Omg WHAT!

Dwayne R: SHE hasn't done anything!!!

Veronica J: Abernathy is my favorite teacher.

Billy S: She's the best.

Aaliyah F: This definitely isn't her fault.

Elise M: Billy, tell her it's not her fault.

Billy S: I did!

Billy S: Believe me.

Veronica J: I HATE THIS LOL HURRICANES GUY EVEN MORE NOW!

Elise M: SAME.

Aarush B: SAME.

Billy S: SAME.

Dwayne R: SAME.

Hena K: SAME.

Aaliyah F: SAME.

Hunter J: I HEAR HIM NOW!

Veronica J: Where?

Elise M: Where?

Billy S: Where?

Hunter J: By 201.

Veronica J: Ok what if like three or four classrooms in the 100 hallway all slam their doors really loud?

Dwayne R: I thought Abernathy said not to do that.

Dwayne R: I'm in the 100 hallway and I don't want him over here!

Veronica J: EVERYONE SHUT UP DWAYNE HAS A BETTER IDEA

Dwayne R: No I don't!

Veronica J: Then YOU shut up, Dwayne.

Elise M: Ooh, burn!

Aarush B: Hahahaha.

Billy S: He's not by 201.

Hunter J: Wait, what?

Hunter J: Then who's by 201?

Billy S: Idk, but the screamy guy is right here.

Billy S: Right outside of Abernathy's room

Aarush B: Omg

Elise M: Omg

Veronica J: LOL HURRICANES

Veronica J: Billy, what's happening now?

Veronica J: Does anyone else hear really LOL HURRICANES loud yelling?

Elise M: Billy?

Hunter J: Billy?

Veronica J: BILLY????????

Battery 2%

TEENBUZZ: WHAT did he just say??? Don't skip these three hot tips on paying closer attention. HINT: It was probably a compliment!

1500+ UNREAD LOLMS NOTIFICATIONS

I think I'm trapped.

E

WHAT

And also HI! You must have found the charger!

CHAR

What do you mean trapped?

I ran past Escott's room and grabbed the charger Elise slid under the door.

But then I heard the intruder guy yelling, so I turned around to run the other way.

THEN, just before I got to the corner, I heard footsteps and scritchy walkie-talkie noises just like in the movies when the SWAT team is sneaking up on a bank robber.

At first, I was like WHEW, the police are here! We're saved!

But THEN I remembered that the second rule of lockdown is to NOT be in the halls when the police are in the halls.

I don't want to accidentally sneak up on THEM.

> How will they know if I'm a good guy or a bad guy?

CHAR

And you're holding a phone. Police don't always realize phones are phones.

> RIGHT?! I watch a LOT of movies AND the actual real news.

> So.

> Now I'm in the janitor's closet and I definitely think I'm trapped.

E

Omg, Ava.

CHAR

Uh. Did the power just go out on you two, too?

E

Yes.

Pitch dark.

> Yes.

> Oh no, oh no, oh no

> I hear footsteps.

What if they see the light from my phone under the door?

I'm turning my phone off.

Love you both.

E

Ava, wait!!

Don't turn your phone off!

Can you turn the brightness way down instead?

We can't help you out of there if your phone is off.

Ava?

CHAR

Ava????

Omg, E, what do we do?

We have to save Ava so she can save Diego!

E

I know, Char! I know!

I can't even think any thoughts right now

I might throw up

Char, I've been fighting it all day, but I think the scared might be winning now.

I feel like I can't breathe.

I don't

I can't

What if?

CHAR

Hey, hey.

I totally get it.

Maybe try taking some deep breaths?

And say to yourself You Are Safe over and over again?

That's what Nurse Shirley helps me do when I'm panicking.

E

But we AREN'T safe, Char.

CHAR

I know. You're totally right.

But . . . you're safe now in the spot where you are, right?

E

I guess?

CHAR

Yes. Good.

Now try this:

Close your eyes.

Take deep breaths.

Pretend like I'm Nurse Shirley telling you this in my calm Nurse Shirley voice:

Tell yourself, *In this Now, I am safe*.

It sounds super dorky, but trust me.

In this Now, I am safe.

In this Now, I am safe.

E

In this Now, I am safe.

CHAR

Good!

E

But what about Ava?

What about Diego?

What about everyone, Char?

CHAR

Just focus on YOU right now, ok?

Moppa always tells me to put my oxygen mask on first.

Like they say on airplanes.

Your mask first. Then help everyone else.

Keep breathing.

Focus.

Put your hands flat on your jeans.

Feel all the little threads and seams.

Keep doing that, ok?

The only things that exist in the world are your breathing and your jeans.

Nurse Shirley taught me the jeans thing last year.

Sometimes it really actually helps.

Feeling better?

E

Better.

CHAR

Good.

Ready to figure out how to save Ava?

E

Yeah.

I'm going to go check the app instead of throwing up.

Maybe everyone on there will have some ideas.

CHAR

You can mix all the ideas together and come up with one great idea.

E

Like a fruit cocktail of ideas?

CHAR

Except fruit cocktail is never great.

But yes. I like the way you're thinking.

E

Thanks, Char.

BRB

LOLMS GLOBAL ANNOUNCEMENTS

Elena K: AVA IS IN TROUBLE.

Elena K: SHE'S HIDING IN A JANITOR'S CLOSET.

Elena K: THE SCREAMY INTRUDER GUY IS ON ONE SIDE OF THE HALL AND THE POLICE ARE ON THE OTHER SIDE.

Elena K: SHE'S TRAPPED.

Elise M: WHAAAAATTTTTTTTT?

Aarush B: OMG

Veronica J: LOL HURRICANES

Elise M: OMG

Billy S: OMG

Elena K: We have to help her get out of there so she can get the inhaler to Diego.

Dwayne R: How can WE do anything?

Veronica J: DO THE DOOR SLAMMING THING. IT'LL BE A DISTRACTION.

Aarush B: Idk. What if those loud bangs sound like OTHER kinds of loud bangs?

Aarush B: That would definitely NOT make it safer in the halls for Ava.

Veronica J: How else can we get the bad guy and the police to leave the hallway?

Elise M: If the screamy guy and the police are really in the same hallway, then they'll arrest him, right?

Elise M: What if Ava just stays put until it's all over, and then gives the inhaler to the police to give to Diego?

Dwayne R: If she does that, then what was even the LOL HURRICANES point of her going out to find the LOL HURRICANES inhaler at all???

Veronica J: IT WAS WORTH A LOL HURRICANES TRY, DWAYNE!

Elena K: Ava said it sounded like the screamy guy and the police were heading in the same direction.

Elena K: I think they're *about* to be in the same hall with her, but they're not there yet. She's trapped because she doesn't know which way to go without being seen.

Billy S: Maybe we're overthinking this. Can't Ava just come out with her hands up and tell the police she's a kid trying to help another kid?

Dwayne R: Maybe on your planet, Billy. Not on my planet.

Aarush B: Not on my planet, either. ESPECIALLY if she has an inhaler or a phone in her hand.

Aarush B: Even if Ava's planet is closer to Billy's, she shouldn't risk it.

Elena K: Well, what are we going to do???? THIS IS A TERRIBLE FRUIT COCKTAIL OF IDEAS, Y'ALL.

Veronica J: ?

Elise M: ?

Billy S: ?

Aarush B: How about this: IF the police and the screamy guy aren't in Ava's hallway yet, maybe there's time for her to get away.

Aarush B: If every classroom lets one kid peek out from under the covered window on their classroom door, then we can all work together to guide Ava away from the bad guy AND the police.

Jung K: Isn't standing near the door against the second rule of lockdown?

Dwayne R: Sometimes we have to LOL HURRICANES do what we have to LOL HURRICANES do, Jung.

Elena K: Then let's hurry up and LOL HURRICANES do it!

E

Ava!

Please, please, please tell me you left your phone on.

Hello?

Ok, hopefully you have the brightness turned down and your phone facedown.

That's what I would do.

Listen:

Everyone is going to work together to guide you out of there, ok?

This is the best fruit cocktail we could make out of all our ideas.

As soon as you see this, go to the app. There's a kid at the door window of every classroom.

They're going to lead you away from, and/or around, the screamy guy and the police.

Don't take any time to respond!

Only look at your screen when you have to!

I'm sure it's still really dark in the hallways without windows, even with the emergency lights.

Don't give yourself away.

Fingers crossed you see this.

Be safe.

Elena K: Ok, let's start with people who can SEE the screamy guy or the police.

Elena K: Tell us which classroom you're in.

Billy S: Abernathy's room. He's down at the corner by Escott's room.

Elise M: Yep. He's at the corner of Escott and the 7th grade bio lab.

Aarush B: From Smith's classroom window, I see a glob of police down by the front office.

Elena K: AVA, THERE IS A BAD GUY IN THE 200 HALLWAY AND A GLOB OF POLICE IN THE 100 HALLWAY.

Elena K: Can anyone tell which way the screamy guy is moving? IS he moving?

Billy S: He's just standing there. Facing the direction of Abernathy's classroom.

Aarush B: The police are huddled together in one spot. No one's going anywhere.

Elena K: AVA YOU SHOULD GO NOW! TOWARD THE 300s!

Aarush B: Can anyone see if Ava's out there? Is she even seeing this?

Li X: She just ran by Anderson's ELA class!

Elena K: YES!

Aarush B: Woo!

Billy S: WAIT! LOL HURRICANES! STOP AVA! The screamy guy just walked past Abernathy's room TOWARD the 300s!!!

Elena K: Nooooo! Let's get her out of there!

Aaliyah F: Ava! Cut through the library to the 500 hallway! It's farther from the art room, but it doesn't connect with the 300 hallway at all.

Elise M: Smart!

Sean P: I can see her! She's running out of the library!

Marcela B: I just saw a glob of police walk into the library!

Aarush B: Omg that was close.

Dwayne R: WHEW

Li X: Yay!

Elena K: Alright. How do we get her from the 500s to the art room?

Veronica J: There are two doors into the girls' locker room.

Veronica J: One in the 500s and one in the 600s. She could snake through there?

Aarush B: And then from the 600s, she could backtrack past the 6th grade math classes!

Li X: And past the smokers bathroom . . .

Elena K: And BOOM. Art room!

Elena K: LOL HURRICANES genius!

Aarush B: Let us know when you get there, Ava.

Elena K: GO, AVA! YOU CAN DO IT!

Li X: You can do it!

Veronica J: You're a LOL HURRICANES ninja!

Dwayne R: You're a LOL HURRICANES superhero!

Elena K: You're the LOL HURRICANES cherry in our LOL HURRICANES fruit cocktail!

4:24 PM

Battery: 19%

LOCAL NEWS TODAY: Parents swarm Lila O'Lowry Middle School as police remain quiet on details.

2000+ UNREAD LOLMS NOTIFICATIONS

E & CHAR

Today 4:25 PM

> Omg I can't believe that worked!

> Diego has the inhaler.

> Ms. Nichols is about to chew my head off.

> Totally worth it, though.

CHAR

Omg I didn't realize I was holding my breath until just now.

E

Saaaaaame.

CHAR

Does Diego seem ok now?

> Yes!

> And oh !

> I got so busy I just now remembered the beacons and pings and uh-oh.

E

Huh?

> BRB

142

MAMABEAR & DADDIO

Today 4:29 PM

Ding, ding! Hi! 😨

Did you know there is no submarine emoji?

[submarine beacon emoji goes here]

MAMABEAR

Ava!!!!!

DADDIO

This isn't the Ava-beacon timeline we anticipated, kiddo.

MAMABEAR

You didn't reassure us AT all.

DADDIO

AND you were not, in fact, back in a sneeze.

Sorry, sorry.

I know that took ... a minute.

I got kind of busy.

Hang on, E is texting.

MAMABEAR

Hang on???

DADDIO

Omg.

4:47 PM

Battery 25%

NATIONAL NEWS NOW: Middle school lockdown escalates as unnamed teacher remains in building. Can police handle unhinged teacher better than llamas? TUNE IN.

LOCAL NEWS TODAY: BREAKING: Police have cut the power and entered LOLMS in search of armed intruder.

TEENBUZZ: Is it possible to have TOO MUCH confidence? Ask our experts!

2300+ UNREAD LOLMS NOTIFICATIONS

LOLMS GLOBAL ANNOUNCEMENTS

Ava McD: Hey, everybody, it's Ava McDaniels. I'm safe in the art room with Diego.

Ava McD: So . . . does anyone know how to mark all the unread comments as read?

Veronica J: AVA!!!!!!

Elise M: AVA!

Katy P: AVA

Billy S: ava!!!!

Li X: AVA

Tom C: AVA!

Jodi E: Omg AVA

Ava S: AVAAAAAAAAA

Marcela B: AVA!!!!!!

Darryl N: Avavavavava!!!

Katie McN: AVA!!!

Ava B: AVA!

Davy F: AvA!!

Jenny M: AVaaaaaaaa!!

Amy P: AVA!!

DeAndre R: AVA!

Javier G: Ava!!!!

Sam R: Ava!

Ike S: AVA?

Georgia K: AVA!

Ava McD: Thank you SOOOOO much for everything, everyone.

Ava McD: And, uh, hi?

Ava McD: Seriously. I could have never done ANY of this without you.

Ava McD: And thank you so much for the charger, Elise.

Ava McD: And thank you for the inhaler, Gabriel. Sorry I crushed it.

Gabriel F: That's ok. I have a million of them.

Dwyane R: YEAH YOU LOL HURRICANES CRUSHED IT. LOOK AT YOU, SUPERHERO!

Veronica J: Hang on. What is THAT? Can you all hear it? That do you all hear really loud banging?

Billy S: Yeah. Someone's banging on the classroom door.

Billy S: like really, really, really hard.

Marcela B: Omg

Elise M: Omg

Aarush B: LOL HURRICANES

Dwayne R: Is it the intruder guy?

Dwayne R: DON'T LET HIM IN.

Veronica J: DUH, DWYANE!

Dwayne R: SHUT UP, VERONICA.

Billy S: It's a guy yelling LOL, LOL, LOL.

Li X: Wait, what?

Ava McD: What?

E & CHAR

Today 4:52 PM

CHAR

If we get out of this, Moppa wants to bake you a cake, btw.

For helping BabyD.

E

WHEN we get out of this.

WHEN.

WHEN.

CHAR

Yes, yes, yes.

When.

Totally when.

Not if.

Never if.

What kind of cake?

CHAR

Idk

Probably whatever kind you want.

There's banging on the art room door now.

And a guy yelling, LOL, LOL, LOL.

Omg WHAT IS GOING ON?

A GUY YELLING LOL LOL WHILE BANGING ON A LOCKED DOOR IS LITERALLY THE OPPOSITE WAY TO MAKE ANYONE LOL OR WANT TO OPEN THE DOOR.

E

It's the police, Ava!

LOL is the codeword so we know to open the door.

You REALLY have to start checking the app.

149

5:13 PM

Battery 30%

NATIONAL NEWS NOW: Watch LIVE as NChopperNow retreats, offering airspace to police helicopter circling Lila O'Lowry Middle School. Unnamed teacher and llamas remain at large.

LOCAL NEWS TODAY: Police confirm armed man entered LOLMS just after 11:30 this morning, looking for his estranged ex-wife, a teacher at the school.

TEENBUZZ: Can YOU tell the difference between dating violence and just a bad mood? WE can!

100+ UNREAD LOLMS NOTIFICATIONS

LOLMS GLOBAL UPDATE

The intruder has been apprehended and police are going room-to-room to evacuate students. The police are using the password "LOL" so that you know it's safe to open the door.

Posted by Principal Nichols today, 5:10 PM

Comments turned off on this post

7:30 PM

Battery 89%

NATIONAL NEWS NOW: Worried by ex-wife's silence, husband searches school and finds . . . llamas? No! He finds HIMSELF arrested!

LOCAL NEWS TODAY: All students and staff are safe after harrowing daylong lockdown ends with school intruder's arrest.

Today 7:31 PM

Everyone ok?

CHAR
Yes, but no.

E
Not really, but yes.

Same

E
That was

…

CHAR
Really scary?

The worst?

E
Yeah.

CHAR
Yeah.

Yeah.

I wish we were together right now and not on our phones.

E

Me too.

CHAR

Same.

Hmm.

I have an idea.

BRB.

8:30 PM

Battery 90%

NATIONAL NEWS NOW: Did today's lockdown at a small-town school endanger students MORE than the intruder? Our panel of experts weight in.

LOCAL NEWS TODAY: Police and teachers hail Lila O'Lowry Middle School students as heroes for protecting beloved teacher "at all costs."

TEENBUZZ: Now you CAN know what he's thinking! Introducing our new daily news feed: TEEN SCENE: A BOY'S POV. You can FINALLY see the world through HIS eyes!

LOLMS: URGENT CHECK THE APP

250+ UNREAD LOLMS NOTIFICATIONS

LOLMS GLOBAL ANNOUNCEMENTS

**ATTENTION ALL STUDENTS AND STAFF:
THERE WILL BE NO SCHOOL TOMORROW.**

SCHOOL WILL RESUME MONDAY.

I am proud beyond words of each and every one of you. Today was a tremendous example of LOL Hurricane pride and togetherness. I want to personally thank each of you for your bravery today. I hope you can all enjoy a safe and quiet weekend.

LOL pride forever,

Principal Nichols

PS If you're still feeling a little scared or uncertain on Monday, be sure to stop by Nurse Shirley's office. The district is providing trauma counselors until the end of next week, so be sure to check the App for the specific times they'll be at school.

Posted by Principal Nichols today, 8:15 PM

Comments turned off on this post

EVERYONE

Today 8:33 PM

Ava renamed this group Check the Texts

Ava renamed this group Friends & Family

Ava renamed this group Frands & Fam

Ava renamed this group FRAMILY

> I had no idea it would show all the edits I made to the group name! Gah!

CHAR

Ashgsdlfh the group name you chose, though.

[Char laughing and rolling her eyes emoji]

E

Omg Char get a phone with emojis! 😏

CHAR

No way! I have 452852846 hours of battery life.

Unlike some people!

> Har, har, har.

E

Guess who's getting a thousand phone chargers for her birthday?

And for Chrismukkah.

Har, har, har to you too.

BABYD

XD

E

Wait. Omg. Did Moppa give in and get Diego a phone???? That was FAST.

THEA

Indeed I did.

JO

Indeed it was.

Omg I already forgot all the parents were in the group chat.

CHAR

You created the group, goofy! [goofy Ava face]

It's been a long day, give me a break. 😶

JO

Yep. It HAS been a long day.

MEG

So long.

JB

The longest.

MEG

BabyD! Welcome to the world of phones!

BABYD

849

849

TH9

THX

>:(

CHAR

XD

He's still learning the art of the flip text

THEA

Char, can't you hear him shouting?

JO

I can hear him all the way out on the porch.

Charlotte, please. Can you change his name in the group?

He doesn't want to be BabyD.

CHAR

He's going to have to learn to text and ask me himself. [tongue sticking out emoji]

THEA

CHARLOTTE ANNE, DO NOT TEST ME IT HAS BEEN A LONG AND SCARY DAY.

CHAR

Fine. Jeez.

Actually, Ava has to do it because she created the group.

Ava edited BABYD to BIGD

BIGD

Omg yes.

JO

NO

THEA

NO

MEG

Ava. Seriously?

Ava edited BABYD to DIEGO

MEG

Thank you. 🙄

Ava edited MEG to MAMABEAR

Ava edited JB to DADDIO

Ava edited AMY to ELENAMAMA

Ava edited FRED to ELENAPAPA

Ava edited THEA to CHARDMOPPA

Ava edited JO to CHARDMAMI

There. It was weird having all the parent names. Fixed it.

E

Or we could just not have parents in this group.

Kidding.

ELENAMAMA

Just piping in to say thank you to Ava for setting up this group.

E

Mom. No. Don't say piping in.

ELENAMAMA

What?

E

Mom omg.

MAMABEAR

You get that, too, Amy? It's MOM OMG a hundred times a day.

CHARDMOPPA

Same thing over here, only it's via their mouths instead of their phones.

DADDIO

Oh, it's via Ava's mouth, too. Trust me.

CHARDMOPPA

[squinted eye laughing emoji]

MAMABEAR

Haha that just showed up on my phone spelled out.

Omg!

CHAR

Like moppa like daughter.

E

This group chat isn't going to be a regular thing, right?

Just for emergencies, right?

Right.

CHAR

Right.

DIEGO

Y37

9:07 PM

Battery 94%

NATIONAL NEWS NOW: Authorities investigate why small-town school was placed on lockdown, costing thousands of taxpayer dollars; give up llama hunt.

LOCAL NEWS TODAY: What should YOU do if you encounter a llama on the loose? Our panel of experts weigh in!

300+ UNREAD LOLMS NOTIFICATIONS

I don't really want to go to sleep tonight. Or be alone.

CHAR

Me neither.

E

Maybe we can have a sleepover!

Like, right now?

CHAR

Tonight?

E

Why not?

ELENAMAMA

The thing is, kiddo, I don't really want you out of my sight ever again.

MAMABEAR

Same.

CHARDMOPPA

Same.

CHAR

Haha.

Seriously, though, what if we ALL have a sleepover?

Like our whole families?

CHARDMOPPA

Where?

Well, we *do* have a spare bedroom and a sofa bed.

E

And we have an air mattress.

CHAR

And we have those sleeping bags we never use.

Pleeeeaaaassseeeee? Dad? Mom? Can everyone come over tonight?

E

Pleeeeeaaaase?

CHAR

Please!!

DIEGO

Even me?

> Especially you, Diego! I didn't save your life so you could NOT bring all your Ms. Marvels over for me to read. 😒 💀

DIEGO

YES.

MAMABEAR

Ok, ok, hold your horses.

Amy, Thea . . . can you give me a call?

Today 9:29 PM

MAMABEAR

Ok yes fine, let's have a gigantic family sleepover even though it's already 9:30.

CHARDMOPPA

But only because today was scary.

167

ELENAMAMA

Entire family Thursday night sleepovers are for post-emergencies only!

CHAR

Yaaaayyyy!!

It'll be like we're at the lake.

Except there's no lake.

CHAR

And it's not summertime.

Wait.

Are we ACTUALLY about to have a sleepover on a school night????

E

Omg Ava

akjghfajklshgafs 💀

CHECK THE APPPPPP!!

There's no school tomorrow!

CHAR

Even I knew that, and I only get random notifications.

[Char laughing at Ava emoji]

DADDIO

Everyone head over when you want.

Bring some snacks!

Mom, you're staying, too, right?

MAMABEAR

Of course.

Tell you what, I'll go grab some marshmallows while I'm out grabbing my overnight bag. We can make s'mores!

WE'RE GOING TO MAKE S'MORES???

CHARDMOPPA

If any night calls for s'mores, it's tonight.

DADDIO

Everyone bring pillows, too!

E

So what's going to happen to the guy?

CHAR

Awkward transition alert . . .

DIEGO

What guy?

CHAR

The guy at school!

The screamy guy who was hunting down Ms. Abernathy!

I'm more worried about Ms. Abernathy.

E

She's lucky he never found her, isn't she?

DIEGO

The news sad.

E

The news could have been a lot sadder.

DIEGO

No.

News SAID.

He just wnt3d.

To tlk.

CHARDMOPPA

When an estranged ex-husband causes the lockdown of an entire middle school, he doesn't just want to talk, kiddo.

ELENAMAMA

Everyone was very lucky today

E

Lucky??

CHARDMOPPA

Today was terrible, but

Well,

I can't even think about what could have happened.

To you all.

To the other students

To your teachers.

To the school staff.

Especially to Ms. Abernathy.

CHARDMAMI

Thea. Hey.

Why don't you start packing up the air mattress so we can get going?

Maybe grab some extra blankets, too?

CHARDMOPPA

Ok.

Can you come help me, Diego? You too, Char.

See you soon, everyone. 🖤

MAMABEAR

See you soon!

9:43 PM

Battery 97%

NATIONAL NEWS NOW: Llama escapes are ON THE RISE. Tune in NOW for the best ways to protect yourself and your family.

TEENBUZZ: Want to catch his eye without getting dress coded? Jacob from TEEN SCENE explores which shirts have you covered!

350+ UNREAD LOLMS NOTIFICATIONS

CHAR

Almost there.

You are such a goof.

I am literally watching you walk down your driveway.

CHAR

Any minute now.

As long as escaped llamas don't stop traffic.

[squinty eye laughing emoji]

E

They're still on the loose, you know.

They've already made me late once today!

CHAR

I see your car, Elena.

Move quickly crossing the street, Char.

Don't get run over.

THAT would be an upsetting ending to an already upsetting day.

E

Heeeere!

Mom and I stopped for extra s'mores supplies. 🔥

Dad is on his way.

Maybe those therapy llamas really will wander by tonight.

I could totally use a therapy llama right now.

CHAR

You're MY therapy llama, Ava.

YOU'RE my therapy llama, Char.

E

And I'M so glad that the llama drama between you two is over.

Meeeee too.

CHAR

Saaaame.

Meet me in the backyard, ok? I'm going to get the s'mores started.

E

Wait! Don't start! I brought a special ingredient!

I'm coming around back now.

CHAR

[Char laughing until she can't make noise emoji]

What are you two tossing back and forth?

asfgfsilugbisb NOOOOOOOO!

Is that a CAN???

Omg.

You did NOT bring fruit cocktail for the s'mores!

E

Of course I did.

It felt urgent.

12:09 AM

[||||]

Battery 100%

LOCAL NEWS TODAY: Lila O'Lowry Middle School has canceled all classes for Friday. Principal Paula Nichols provided no further comment.

TEENBUZZ: Is your man always grouchy? Try these new tricks to turn his frown upside down!

LILA O'LOWRY MIDDLE SCHOOL APP: It has been 1 day since you last checked the LOLMS app.

Char?

E is conked out and her snoring totally woke me up.

Did she wake you up, too?

Where'd you go?

CHAR

In the shower.

In the middle of the night?

With your phone?

CHAR

It's water resistant AND the battery lasts 42959256 hours.

You know water resistant isn't the same as waterproof, right?

CHAR

Yes it is! Isn't it? Uh-oh.

Why are you in the shower?

CHAR

It calms me down.

I like to feel the hot prickles.

Like ... when you can't get enough tears to squeeze from your eyes.

A burning hot shower feels kind of like tears raining down on your whole body.

Plus, I like the sound of it.

It drowns out all the other thoughts in my head.

Are you ok?

You don't really sound ok?

Want me to get Moppa?

CHAR

I know it sounds weird, but I'm ok.

I'm going to stay in here for a bit, though.

It was a long, bad day, Ava.

Even though we're all safe and everything, I just ...

I 10000000% get it.

You don't have to explain to me at all.

Stay in there as long as you need.

Text me if you need me.

Love you.

CHAR

Love you, too, Ava.

3:43 AM

Battery 100%

Do Not Disturb

Are you asleep?

E

I'm right next to you staring at you stare at your phone.

CHAR

It's so bright omg

Didn't you learn something about screen brightness today?

Hmm?

har, har.

We really are lucky, aren't we?

CHAR

Yeah.

E

We really are.

I hope Ms. Abernathy is with friends tonight, too.

CHAR

I hope they're helping her feel safe

E

And loved.

Maybe the llamas went to her house and that's why they didn't come here.

E

I sure hope so.

CHAR

Me too.

[heart emoji]

[llama emoji]

[heart emoji]

About the Author

K. A. Holt is the award-winning author of many middle-grade novels in verse including *BenBee and the Teacher Griefer*, *Redwood and Ponytail*, *Knockout*, *House Arrest*, and *Rhyme Schemer*. She is also the author of *From You to Me*, *Gnome-a-geddon*, and several other books for young readers, including *I Wonder*, a picture book illustrated by Kenard Pak. K. A. lives in Austin, Texas.